STAR WARS™

THE RISE OF A HERO

WRITTEN BY
LOUISE SIMONSON

ART BY
**WALTER SIMONSON,
TOM PALMER, AND LAURA MARTIN**

PRINTED IN THE UNITED STATES OF AMERICA
FIRST EDITION, MAY 2017
1 3 5 7 9 10 8 6 4 2
LIBRARY OF CONGRESS CONTROL NUMBER ON FILE
FAC-038091-17104
ISBN 978-1-4847-9933-8

VISIT THE OFFICIAL *STAR WARS* WEBSITE AT: WWW.STARWARS.COM.

DISNEP
LUCASFILM
P R E S S
LOS ANGELES · NEW YORK

SUSTAINABLE FORESTRY INITIATIVE
Certified Sourcing
www.sfiprogram.org
SFI-00993
Logo Applies to Text Stock Only

LUKE SKYWALKER STREAKS THROUGH THE HOT DESERT WORLD OF *TATOOINE* IN HIS SLEEK LANDSPEEDER. HE'S RACING TO SEE HIS BEST FRIEND, *BIGGS DARKLIGHTER*, WHO LEFT FOR THE ACADEMY THE YEAR BEFORE.

NOW BIGGS IS HOME FOR A VISIT, AND LUKE WANTS TO HEAR ALL ABOUT HIS EXPLOITS.

BUT INSTEAD BIGGS TELLS HIM A *DANGEROUS SECRET:* HE'S GOING TO LEAVE SCHOOL AND JOIN THE REBELLION.

THE REBELLION! EVEN THE MOISTURE FARMERS OF TATOOINE HAVE EXPERIENCED THE EVILS OF THE *GALACTIC EMPIRE*, AND LUKE WANTS DESPERATELY TO BE A PART OF THE FIGHT.

BUT HE REALIZES THAT IS UNLIKELY. NOTHING EXCITING *EVER* HAPPENS NEAR TATOOINE. ON THIS DRY AND DUSTY WORLD, IT'S NEARLY IMPOSSIBLE TO KEEP HUMAN WORKERS. EVEN PEOPLE LIKE BIGGS WHO GREW UP ON TATOOINE FLEE THE *BORING PLANET* AS SOON AS POSSIBLE. BUT LUKE IS STUCK HERE, WORKING ON HIS UNCLE'S MOISTURE FARM—GOING NOWHERE.

JAWA *SCAVENGERS* OFFER DROIDS FOR SALE. UNCLE OWEN PICKS *C-3PO*, A TALKATIVE *PROTOCOL DROID* WHO WILL WORK WELL WITH OWEN'S OTHER EQUIPMENT. THEN HE CHOOSES A SMALL RED ROBOT. BUT AS OWEN IS ABOUT TO PAY, THAT ROBOT *MALFUNCTIONS.*

THREEPIO POINTS AT A LITTLE BLUE *ASTROMECH DROID.* "ARTOO IS IN PERFECT CONDITION!" HE TELLS LUKE. SO UNCLE OWEN BUYS *R2-D2* INSTEAD, UNAWARE OF HOW THESE DROIDS WILL FOREVER CHANGE THEIR LIVES—AND THE LIVES OF *EVERYONE IN THE GALAXY.*

LUKE LEADS THE DROIDS TO THE GARAGE TO CLEAN THEM. AN OIL BATH RINSES THE SCRATCHY SAND FROM THREEPIO'S JOINTS. BUT ARTOO IS SOOTY, AS THOUGH HE'S BEEN IN *BATTLE.* HE EVEN HAS A PIECE OF METAL JAMMED INTO HIS NECK CREVICE!

LUKE TRIES TO PRY IT OUT. WITH A STARTLED CRY, HE STUMBLES BACKWARD AS A *HOLOGRAM* OF A BEAUTIFUL GIRL APPEARS! OVER AND OVER, SHE PLEADS, "HELP ME, OBI-WAN KENOBI. *YOU'RE MY ONLY HOPE.*"

LUKE IS SURE THERE'S MORE TO THE MESSAGE, BUT ARTOO WON'T PLAY IT. THE DROID WHIRS AND BEEPS, INSISTING THE MESSAGE IS *PRIVATE* AND THAT HE IS THE PROPERTY OF OBI-WAN!

THAT EVENING LUKE ASKS HIS UNCLE IF THE MESSAGE COULD BE FOR *BEN KENOBI,* AN OLD HERMIT WHO LIVES FAR OUT ON THE *DUNE SEA.* MAYBE ARTOO WAS STOLEN FROM HIM.

UNCLE OWEN SCOWLS. "OLD BEN DOESN'T EXIST ANYMORE," HE MUTTERS. "ARTOO IS OUR DROID NOW. TAKE HIM INTO TOWN TOMORROW AND HAVE HIS *MEMORY ERASED.*"

LUKE'S PARENTS ARE DEAD, BUT HE KNOWS HIS AUNT AND UNCLE LOVE HIM. HE ALSO KNOWS THEY NEED HIS HELP. BUT HE DESPERATELY WANTS TO *LEAVE* THIS DESERT WORLD.

UNCLE OWEN SHAKES HIS HEAD. "MAYBE NEXT YEAR," HE SAYS. LUKE SIGHS, KNOWING FROM EXPERIENCE THAT NEXT YEAR *NEVER* SEEMS TO COME.

THE SETTING SUNS SPILL LIGHT ACROSS THE SAND, BUT LUKE IS IN NO MOOD TO APPRECIATE THE PLANET'S ARID BEAUTY. THREEPIO IS *CONCERNED.* "ARTOO IS MALFUNCTIONING. HE'S GONE TO LOOK FOR OBI-WAN." BUT IT'S TOO *DANGEROUS* TO SEARCH FOR THE DROID AT NIGHT.

THE NEXT MORNING, LUKE SCANS THE LANDSCAPE FRANTICALLY, FINALLY SPOTTING ARTOO'S TRACKS. HE LEAPS INTO HIS *LANDSPEEDER* AND HAULS THREEPIO IN AFTER HIM. AT BREAKNECK SPEED, THEY *ZOOM* AFTER THE RUNAWAY DROID!

LUKE IS NEARLY AS WORRIED ABOUT ARTOO'S SAFETY AS HE IS ABOUT THE TROUBLE HE COULD BE IN HIMSELF. THE *JUNDLAND WASTES* ARE FILLED WITH JAWAS WHO COULD STEAL THE ECCENTRIC LITTLE DROID. AND THE TERRIFYING *TUSKEN RAIDERS*—FIERCE NOMADIC SAND PEOPLE WHO HAVE BEEN RAIDING LOCAL FARMS—COULD SET THEIR SIGHTS ON LUKE.

FINALLY, IN A ROCKY CANYON, LUKE SPOTS THE DELINQUENT DROID. AS LUKE LEAPS FROM HIS LANDSPEEDER, ARTOO WHISTLES AND ROCKS EXCITEDLY.
   LUKE DOESN'T UNDERSTAND WHAT HE'S TRYING TO TELL HIM . . . UNTIL IT IS *TOO LATE.*

SLOWLY, LUKE REGAINS CONSCIOUSNESS. HE SQUINTS UP INTO THE WEATHERED FACE OF *OLD BEN KENOBI*. "THIS LITTLE DROID IS SEARCHING FOR HIS FORMER MASTER, AN OBI-WAN KENOBI," LUKE MUMBLES. "DO YOU KNOW HIM?"

THE OLD MAN SMILES. "OBI-WAN? I HAVEN'T GONE BY THE NAME OBI-WAN SINCE BEFORE YOU WERE BORN."

SO OLD BEN KENOBI *IS* OBI-WAN!

AS LUKE STANDS SHAKILY, THE OLD MAN SAYS HE DROVE OFF THE SAND PEOPLE WHO *ATTACKED* LUKE AND THE DROIDS BUT THEY WILL *SOON RETURN*. HE INVITES LUKE TO HIS HOME, WHERE THEY CAN SPEAK SAFELY.

BEN ALSO HAS SOMETHING THERE TO GIVE HIM.

ONCE INSIDE, BEN HANDS LUKE A SILVER CYLINDER. "THIS IS YOUR *FATHER'S LIGHTSABER*, THE WEAPON OF A *JEDI KNIGHT*," HE SAYS. LUKE PRESSES A BUTTON AND, WITH A HUM, AN ENERGY BLADE FLARES FROM ITS TIP.

THEN BEN TELLS LUKE MANY THINGS HE DID NOT KNOW.

LUKE'S FATHER WAS A JEDI KNIGHT, ONE OF THE *GUARDIANS OF PEACE AND JUSTICE* IN THE OLD REPUBLIC. HE WAS BETRAYED BY A YOUNG JEDI NAMED *DARTH VADER*.

VADER WAS SEDUCED BY THE DARK SIDE OF THE *FORCE*.

BEN EXPLAINS THAT THE FORCE IS AN ENERGY FIELD THAT GIVES JEDI THEIR POWER.

IT SURROUNDS ALL THINGS AND BINDS THE GALAXY TOGETHER, AND CAN BE USED FOR *GOOD* OR FOR *EVIL*.

LONG AGO, DARTH VADER CHOSE EVIL. AT THE COMMAND OF THE *EMPEROR*, HE HUNTED DOWN AND DESTROYED MOST OF THE JEDI, INCLUDING *LUKE'S FATHER*.

THEN, AT BEN'S REQUEST, ARTOO PLAYS BACK THE ENTIRE *SECRET MESSAGE*.

THIS TIME, LUKE SEES THE BEAUTIFUL GIRL INSERT A DISC INTO ARTOO. SHE SAYS SHE IS ABOUT TO BE CAPTURED BUT HAS PLACED IMPORTANT INFORMATION IN THE DROID. SHE *BEGS* OBI-WAN TO TAKE THE DROID TO HER FATHER. THE INFORMATION ARTOO CARRIES COULD SAVE THE REBELLION.

BEN EXPLAINS THAT SHE IS *PRINCESS LEIA ORGANA* OF ALDERAAN. HE ASKS LUKE TO COME WITH HIM, TO STUDY AND BECOME A JEDI LIKE HIS FATHER. HE TELLS LUKE THAT PRINCESS LEIA NEEDS HIM.

LUKE WANTS TO GO, BUT HE CAN'T ABANDON HIS AUNT AND UNCLE. INSTEAD, HE OFFERS TO TAKE BEN TO THE *MOS EISLEY SPACEPORT*, WHERE THE OLD MAN CAN GET ON A SHIP TO *ALDERAAN*.

SPEEDING THROUGH THE ARID WASTE, THEY DISCOVER THE *SMOKING RUIN* OF A *SANDCRAWLER.* SLAIN JAWAS LIE BESIDE IT. *THESE ARE THE JAWAS WHO SOLD US ARTOO AND THREEPIO!* LUKE REALIZES. WHY WOULD SAND PEOPLE ATTACK THEM?

BEN STUDIES THE SMOLDERING RUBBLE. "IT *WASN'T* SAND PEOPLE," HE SAYS. "*IMPERIAL STORMTROOPERS* DID THIS. THEY MUST HAVE BEEN AFTER THESE DROIDS."

LUKE HAS A *TERRIBLE* THOUGHT: *WHAT IF THE STORMTROOPERS LEARNED MY UNCLE BOUGHT THE DROIDS? WHAT WOULD THEY DO TO HIM?* DESPERATELY, LUKE RACES TOWARD THE FARM.

LUKE'S HOME IS A CHARRED RUIN. HIS AUNT AND UNCLE ARE DEAD. STARING AT THE DREADFUL DEVASTATION, HE KNOWS THERE IS NO LONGER ANY REASON TO REMAIN ON TATOOINE—AND *ONE* VERY IMPORTANT REASON TO LEAVE.

LUKE TURNS TO BEN. "I WANT TO GO WITH YOU TO ALDERAAN," HE SAYS GRIMLY. "I WANT TO LEARN THE WAYS OF THE FORCE AND BECOME A *JEDI* LIKE MY FATHER."

WHEN THEY REACH MOS EISLEY SPACEPORT, **STORMTROOPERS** ARE STOPPING EVERY VEHICLE, SEARCHING FOR THE MISSING DROIDS.

LUKE IS WORRIED, BUT WHEN THE STORMTROOPERS STUDY ARTOO AND THREEPIO, BEN MURMURS, "THESE **AREN'T** THE DROIDS YOU'RE LOOKING FOR."

THE MESMERIZED SQUADRON LEADER SAYS, "THESE AREN'T THE DROIDS WE'RE LOOKING FOR," AND WAVES THEM ON.

LUKE GAPES, BUT BEN SMILES. "THE FORCE CAN HAVE A STRONG INFLUENCE ON THE WEAK-MINDED," HE SAYS.

"YOU WILL FIND IT A POWERFUL ALLY."

LEAVING THE DROIDS OUTSIDE, LUKE AND BEN ENTER THE MOS EISLEY CANTINA, HOPING TO HIRE A **FAST SHIP** AND A **PILOT** WHO WON'T ASK QUESTIONS.

WHILE BEN SPEAKS TO *CHEWBACCA*, THE WOOKIEE FIRST MATE ON A SMUGGLING SHIP CALLED THE *MILLENNIUM FALCON*, AN ALIEN TOUGH TRIES TO START A FIGHT WITH LUKE.

BEN FLASHES HIS LIGHTSABER, AND IN AN INSTANT, THE FIGHT IS *OVER.* IT MAKES LUKE WANT MORE THAN EVER TO BE A JEDI.

HAN SOLO, THE SHIP'S CAPTAIN, BOASTS THAT THE *FALCON* IS SO FAST IT CAN OUTRUN HUGE IMPERIAL STARSHIPS.

CAN THAT *BE TRUE?* LUKE WONDERS. IF SO, HAN MUST HAVE ONE INCREDIBLE SHIP!

THEY AGREE TO PAY HAN A SMALL FEE WHEN THEY BOARD AND MUCH MORE WHEN THEY ARRIVE ON ALDERAAN. LUKE OFFERS TO SELL HIS LANDSPEEDER TO MAKE THE DOWN PAYMENT. HE'S *NEVER* COMING BACK TO TATOOINE ANYWAY.

AFTER THE SALE, LUKE HANDS BEN THE CREDITS. THEY ENTER THE SPACEPORT, *UNAWARE* THAT THEY HAVE BEEN SPOTTED.

LUKE DOESN'T KNOW WHAT HE'S BEEN EXPECTING THE *MILLENNIUM FALCON* TO LOOK LIKE, BUT THE ANCIENT PIECE OF *JUNK* IN DOCKING BAY NINETY-FOUR IS *NOTHING* LIKE IT!

"SHE MAY NOT LOOK LIKE MUCH, BUT SHE'S GOT IT WHERE IT *COUNTS*, KID," HAN GROWLS AS HE HURRIES THEM ON BOARD. THE DOOR IS ALMOST CLOSED WHEN HAN SPOTS *TROUBLE*. "CHEWIE, GET US OUT OF HERE!" HE YELLS.

WITH A *ROAR* OF ITS MIGHTY ENGINES, THE *MILLENNIUM FALCON* LEAPS TOWARD SPACE. THE STORMTROOPERS BELOW CAN DO NOTHING TO STOP THEM.

THEY'VE ESCAPED! LUKE
SIGHS WITH RELIEF, UNTIL
HUGE BLASTS ROCK THE SHIP.
IMPERIAL CRUISERS ARE
CLOSING IN ON THEM!

"WHY DON'T YOU OUTRUN
THEM?" LUKE YELLS AT HAN.
"YOU SAID THIS THING IS FAST."

AS HAN STEERS FRANTICALLY,
HE GROWLS, "I JUST NEED THE

FINAL COORDINATES. WE'LL BE
SAFE ENOUGH ONCE WE MAKE
THE JUMP TO *HYPERSPACE*!"

STARS BECOME SHIMMERING
STREAKS, AND IN AN INSTANT
THE *MILLENNIUM FALCON*
IS SOMEWHERE ELSE. THE
OTHERS TAKE IT IN STRIDE, BUT
LUKE HAS NEVER EXPERIENCED
ANYTHING SO EXHILARATING.

HIS BORING DAYS AS A FARM BOY ARE FINALLY OVER!

THEY HAVE SOME TIME BEFORE THEY REACH ALDERAAN. WHILE ARTOO AND CHEWIE PLAY A GAME AND HAN MAKES REPAIRS, BEN BEGINS TO TEACH LUKE HOW TO WIELD HIS LIGHTSABER . . .

AND HOW TO USE THE FORCE.

BEN TELLS LUKE TO DEFLECT THE SHOTS OF THE FLOATING TRAINING REMOTE WITH THE LIGHTSABER BLADE, BUT IT'S *HARDER* THAN IT LOOKS.

NO MATTER HOW CAREFULLY LUKE AIMS, HE MISSES. THE REMOTE ZAPS HIM EVERY TIME. BUT THIS JUST MAKES HIM MORE DETERMINED TO MASTER THE JEDI WEAPON.

SUDDENLY, BEN SLUMPS INTO A CHAIR. "I FELT A GREAT DISTURBANCE IN THE FORCE," HE EXPLAINS, "AS IF MILLIONS OF VOICES CRIED OUT IN TERROR AND WERE SUDDENLY SILENCED. *"I FEAR SOMETHING TERRIBLE HAS HAPPENED."*

NOW IT IS MORE IMPORTANT THAN EVER THAT LUKE CONTINUES HIS JEDI TRAINING—AND ESPECIALLY THAT HE LEARNS TO USE THE FORCE. BEN HANDS HIM A *HELMET* WITH A *BLAST SHIELD* THAT COMPLETELY COVERS HIS EYES.

THIS TIME, HE WANTS LUKE TO *PRACTICE BLIND.*

BEN SAYS A JEDI CAN FEEL THE FORCE FLOWING THROUGH HIM. HE TELLS LUKE TO LET GO OF HIS CONSCIOUS SELF AND ACT ON INSTINCT. "YOUR EYES CAN DECEIVE YOU. *DON'T* TRUST THEM," HE SAYS. "STRETCH OUT WITH YOUR FEELINGS."

LUKE REACHES OUT WITH HIS SENSES AND *BLOCKS* THE THREE SHOTS! BUT BEFORE HE CAN TRY AGAIN, HAN CALLS OUT, "WE'RE COMING UP ON ALDERAAN."

LUKE RUSHES TO THE COCKPIT,
EAGER TO GET A LOOK AT THIS
NEW PLANET, BUT ALL HE SEES
ARE GIANT WHIRLING ROCKS!
"WHERE IS IT?" HE ASKS.
  "IT AIN'T HERE," HAN GROWLS.
  "IT HAS BEEN *DESTROYED* . . .
BY THE *EMPIRE*," BEN SAYS.
  DESTROYED? LUKE CAN HARDLY
BELIEVE IT. HOW COULD *ANY*
WEAPON BE POWERFUL ENOUGH
TO SHATTER A PLANET?

THEY DRIFT THROUGH TUMBLING ROCKS AND DEBRIS, THE
WRECKAGE OF A WORLD AND ALL THAT REMAINS OF PRINCESS
LEIA'S HOME. THE ONLY THING INTACT IS *A SMALL MOON.*
  AS THE *MILLENNIUM FALCON* FLIES CLOSER TO INVESTIGATE, BEN
REALIZES IT *ISN'T* A MOON AT ALL.
  "TURN THE SHIP AROUND!" BEN SHOUTS.

HAN TRIES, BUT ESCAPE IS IMPOSSIBLE. A *TRACTOR BEAM* HAS LOCKED ON TO THE DEFENSELESS SHIP AND IS DRAGGING IT TOWARD AN OPEN DOCKING PORT IN THE EVIL EMPIRE'S BEHEMOTH BATTLE STATION, THE *DEATH STAR.*

WHEN TWO STORMTROOPERS BOARD THE *MILLENNIUM FALCON*, HAN POUNCES. *DISGUISED* IN THE DEFEATED STORMTROOPERS' ARMOR, HAN AND LUKE LEAVE THE SHIP, PRETENDING TO ESCORT THE OTHERS AS THEIR PRISONERS.

STEALTHILY, THEY SLIP INTO AN EMPTY COMMAND ROOM, WHERE ARTOO PLUGS INTO A *CONTROL PANEL*. INSTANTLY, HE ACCESSES THE IMPERIAL COMPUTER NETWORK.

WHEN ARTOO LOCATES THE TRACTOR BEAM CONTROL, BEN SETS OUT TO DEACTIVATE IT, ORDERING THE OTHERS TO STAY WHERE THEY ARE.

BUT THEN ARTOO FINDS *PRINCESS LEIA*! SHE'S IN THE BATTLE STATION, ON THE PRISON LEVEL. LUKE KNOWS THEY HAVE TO *RESCUE HER.*

QUICKLY, HE TELLS THE OTHERS HIS *PLAN*. THE DROIDS WILL STAY BEHIND WHILE LUKE AND HAN PRETEND TO ESCORT CHEWBACCA TO THE PRISON LEVEL. ONCE THERE, THEY'LL LOCATE LEIA AND LIBERATE HER!

HAN AGREES BUT ONLY WHEN LUKE PROMISES HIM A HUGE *REWARD*. AFTER ALL, THEY WILL BE RESCUING A PRINCESS, AND AS EVERYONE KNOWS, PRINCESSES ARE *RICH*!

LUKE'S CLEVER PLAN TAKES THEM AS FAR AS THE PRISON LEVEL, BUT THERE THEY RUN INTO *TROUBLE*. HAN AND CHEWBACCA FIGHT OFF ATTACKING STORMTROOPERS WHILE LUKE RUSHES TO RELEASE THE PRINCESS.

LUKE **BLASTS** THE LOCK AND **BURSTS** INTO HER CELL. "I'M LUKE SKYWALKER," HE GASPS. "I'M HERE TO RESCUE YOU. I'VE GOT YOUR R2 UNIT. I'M HERE WITH BEN KENOBI."

PRINCESS LEIA LEAPS TO HER FEET. THAT'S ALL SHE NEEDS TO HEAR.

BUT AS THEY RUSH FROM THE CELL, HAN AND CHEWBACCA ARE RACING TOWARD THEM, DODGING **LASER BLASTS**. WITH IRATE STORMTROOPERS ON THEIR TAILS, THE HEROES ARE **TRAPPED IN THE CELL BAY**.

BUT LEIA **ISN'T** THE SORT OF PRINCESS WHO SIMPLY **WAITS** TO BE RESCUED.

PRINCESS LEIA SNATCHES
LUKE'S BLASTER AND *SHOOTS*
THROUGH A GRATE IN THE WALL.
AT FIRST LUKE DOESN'T
UNDERSTAND WHAT SHE'S

DOING. THEN HE GETS IT! THE
GRATE OPENS INTO A SHAFT.
THEY CAN SLIDE DOWN THE
PASSAGE AND *ESCAPE!*

LEIA, LUKE, CHEWIE, AND
FINALLY HAN DIVE INTO THE
HOLE. THEY LAND IN A PILE
OF *REEKING GARBAGE*,
SURROUNDED BY LIQUID
SLUDGE . . .
    AND IN EVEN MORE *TROUBLE*.

INSIDE THE GARBAGE ROOM,
A *SLIMY TENTACLE* DRAGS
LUKE BENEATH THE SCUMMY
SEWAGE. HAN FIRES, BUT
HIS BLASTS *DON'T* STOP
THE MONSTER. FOR A LONG
MOMENT, LUKE IS GONE.

THEN, WITH A DEEP RUMBLE,
THE ROOM BEGINS TO *SHAKE*.
SUDDENLY, LUKE BOBS TO THE
SURFACE. THE MONSTER HAS
RELEASED HIM.
    BUT WHY?

THE WALLS OF THE ROOM START TO SLIDE TOGETHER. LUKE REALIZES THEY ARE CAUGHT IN A HUGE *TRASH MASHER.* NORMALLY, IT JUST CRUSHES GARBAGE. NOW IT IS ABOUT TO *CRUSH THEM!*

AS THEY TRY TO BRACE THE WALLS, LUKE SHOUTS INTO HIS *COMLINK,* TELLING THREEPIO TO TURN OFF ALL THE GARBAGE MASHERS ON THE PRISON LEVEL.

IT WORKS! THE WALLS STOP MOVING, AND THEY ESCAPE INTO ANOTHER CORRIDOR.

LUKE AND HAN ARE STRIPPING OFF THEIR WET AND STINKING ARMOR WHEN, SUDDENLY, MORE STORMTROOPERS ARRIVE.

AND ONCE AGAIN THEY ARE *ON THE RUN.*

BREEP
BOOP

LUKE AND LEIA ARE *TRAPPED*. THERE'S NO WAY TO GET ACROSS. UNLESS . . . LUKE SUDDENLY REMEMBERS THAT HIS UTILITY BELT HOLDS A *GRAPPLING HOOK*! BUT WILL IT WORK?

WHILE LEIA HOLDS OFF THE STORMTROOPERS, LUKE HURLS THE HOOK ACROSS THE CHASM. IT CATCHES, AND THE LINE PULLS TIGHT.

LEIA GIVES LUKE A QUICK KISS FOR LUCK. THEN THEY'RE *SWINGING* ACROSS THE VAST ABYSS TO SAFETY ON THE OTHER SIDE!

PEW PEW

WHEN LUKE AND LEIA REACH THE DOCKING BAY, HAN AND CHEWIE ARE WAITING IN THE SHADOWS. ACROSS THE BAY, *LIGHTSABERS ARE CLASHING* AS STORMTROOPERS WATCH WITH FASCINATION.

"IT'S BEN!" LUKE WHISPERS.

LEIA NODS. "AND HE'S *FIGHTING DARTH VADER!*"

DARTH VADER, LUKE THINKS.

THE IMPERIAL MONSTER WHO DESTROYED MY FATHER!

THE BLADES CONTINUE TO FLASH AS THE ENEMIES FACE OFF IN A *SAVAGE DUEL*, AND IT IS CLEAR THIS BATTLE WILL END ONLY WHEN ONE OF THEM IS *DEAD*. THOUGH BEN IS OLD AND WITHOUT ARMOR, HE MATCHES THE ARMORED GIANT BLOW FOR BLOW.

THEN BEN SPOTS LUKE AND THE OTHERS AND SOMETHING *STRANGE* HAPPENS. HE LIFTS HIS SWORD AND STEPS BACK. HE LETS DARTH VADER SLASH RIGHT THROUGH HIM! BEN'S ROBE FALLS TO THE FLOOR, BUT IT'S . . . *EMPTY*. BEN IS GONE.

IN HORROR, LUKE *SCREAMS* BEN'S NAME. THE STORMTROOPERS WHIRL AND OPEN FIRE. THAT'S WHEN LUKE THINKS HE HEARS BEN CALLING TO HIM: *RUN, LUKE! RUN!*

AS THEY *DASH* FOR THE SHIP, HAN MUTTERS, "I JUST HOPE THE OLD MAN MANAGED TO TURN OFF THE TRACTOR BEAM!"

OBI-WAN KENOBI IS GONE, BUT HE KEPT HIS PROMISE. THE TRACTOR BEAM IS OFF. THE *MILLENNIUM FALCON* CAN *ESCAPE INTO SPACE.*

LUKE FEELS THE LOSS OF BEN GREATLY. HIS AUNT AND UNCLE ARE DEAD. NOW HIS TEACHER, WHO HAD ALREADY BEGUN TO FEEL ALMOST LIKE A FATHER, IS GONE, TOO.

BUT THERE'S NO TIME TO GRIEVE. *IMPERIAL TIE FIGHTERS* ARE POURING OUT OF THE BATTLE STATION.

THEY'RE GOING TO HAVE TO *FIGHT FOR THEIR LIVES.*

WHILE CHEWBACCA PILOTS
THE SHIP, LUKE AND HAN MAN
THE *LASER CANNONS*. THEY
FIRE, AGAIN AND AGAIN, UNTIL
ALL THE TIE FIGHTERS ARE
GONE.

HAN AND LUKE ARE EXCITED.
THEY WORKED TOGETHER AND
THEY *WON!* BUT LEIA THINKS

THEIR ESCAPE WAS *TOO EASY.*
SHE'S SURE DARTH VADER LET
THEM GO.

HAN IS *ANNOYED* WITH LEIA,
BUT AS THE *MILLENNIUM
FALCON* JUMPS INTO
HYPERSPACE, LUKE WONDERS
IF SHE MIGHT BE *RIGHT.*

WITH ALDERAAN ANNIHILATED, THEY HAVE NO CHOICE BUT TO FLY TO THE FOURTH MOON OF *YAVIN*, THE MAIN BASE OF THE REBELLION.

ARTOO HOLDS THE *SECRET PLANS* TO THE DEATH STAR, AND LEIA HOPES THE REBEL LEADERS CAN USE THEM TO FIND A WAY TO *DESTROY* THE DEADLY SPACE STATION BEFORE IT THREATENS MORE WORLDS.

LUKE SAW WHAT THE DEATH STAR DID TO ALDERAAN. HE KNOWS THAT FINDING A *WEAKNESS* IN THE SPACE STATION MAY BE THE REBELS' ONLY HOPE.

IN THE WAR ROOM, REBEL PILOTS WATCH CLOSELY AS *GENERAL DODONNA* PROJECTS THE PLANS TO THE BATTLE STATION. HE POINTS TO A *NARROW TRENCH* THAT LEADS TO A SMALL EXHAUST PORT THAT FEEDS DIRECTLY INTO THE REACTOR. IF THEY CAN FIRE A TORPEDO INTO IT, A *CHAIN REACTION* WILL *DESTROY* THE DEATH STAR.

"THAT'S IMPOSSIBLE, EVEN WITH A TARGETING COMPUTER!" WHISPERS *WEDGE ANTILLES*, A PILOT IN LUKE'S RED SQUADRON.

"IT'S *NOT IMPOSSIBLE*. I USED TO BULL'S-EYE WOMP RATS THE SIZE OF THAT PORT FROM MY SKYHOPPER BACK HOME!" LUKE ANSWERS.

ALARMS SOUND, ANNOUNCING THE DEATH STAR'S ARRIVAL ON THE FAR SIDE OF YAVIN 4. THE REBEL PILOTS *RACE* FOR THEIR X-WINGS.

HAN HAS GOTTEN HIS *REWARD*, AND HE AND CHEWBACCA ARE *LEAVING*. HE URGES LUKE TO COME WITH THEM, BUT LUKE HAS SEEN WHAT EVIL THE EMPIRE IS CAPABLE OF AND HE NEEDS TO STOP IT. ANGRILY, LUKE TURNS AWAY FROM HAN.

THEN BIGGS, HIS BEST FRIEND FROM TATOOINE, DASHES UP, EXCITED TO SEE LUKE, GLAD THAT THEY'RE BOTH IN *RED SQUADRON*.

BIGGS IS A LINK TO LUKE'S HOME AND FAMILY. IT FEELS LIKE A *SIGN* EVERYTHING WILL BE ALL RIGHT.

AS LUKE'S *X-WING* SOARS INTO BATTLE, HE THINKS HE HEARS *BEN* SAY, LUKE, THE FORCE WILL BE WITH YOU.

KA-SHOOM

PEW

PEW

PEW

PEW

PEW

CHOOM

EXPLOSIONS *ROCK* THE REBEL FLEET AS IMPERIAL TIE FIGHTERS CLOSE IN.

RED SQUADRON'S ORDERS ARE TO *HOLD OFF* THE TIES AND *PROTECT* GOLD SQUADRON, AND LUKE JOINS THE DOGFIGHT EAGERLY.

BELOW, IN THE DEATH STAR TRENCH, GOLD SQUADRON PILOTS TRY DESPERATELY TO HIT THE EXHAUST PORT. BUT AGAIN AND AGAIN *THEY FAIL.*

THE DEATH STAR IS *POWERING UP*, GETTING READY TO FIRE THE BEAM THAT WILL *DESTROY* YAVIN 4. TIME IS RUNNING OUT.

FINALLY, IT IS UP TO RED SQUADRON. IF THEY FAIL TO MAKE THE SHOT, THE MOON BELOW, AND EVERYONE ON IT, WILL BE *DOOMED*.

SEVERAL MORE EXPERIENCED PILOTS FIRE AND MISS. AND THEN, AT LAST, IT'S *LUKE'S TURN.*

LUKE DROPS INTO THE TRENCH *FULL THROTTLE*, WITH BIGGS
AND WEDGE BEHIND HIM IN TIGHT FORMATION. SUDDENLY, LASER
BOLTS STREAK PAST LUKE AS A *POWERFUL ODDLY SHAPED TIE
FIGHTER*, FOLLOWED BY TWO WINGMEN, SWOOPS IN BEHIND THEM.

BIGGS AND WEDGE FALL BACK TO PROTECT LUKE, BUT PRECISION BLASTS FROM THE STRANGE SHIP KNOCK WEDGE FROM THE TRENCH AND ENGULF BIGGS'S X-WING IN FLAMES.

FINALLY, ONLY LUKE IS LEFT.

LUKE BEGINS TO LINE UP THE SHOT ON HIS TARGETING COMPUTER. THEN HE HEARS BEN'S VOICE AGAIN: *USE THE FORCE, LUKE.*

HE THINKS ABOUT HIS *JEDI TRAINING* ABOARD THE *MILLENNIUM FALCON.* HE REALIZES THE COMPUTERS *HAVEN'T* WORKED FOR ANYONE ELSE AND PROBABLY WON'T WORK FOR HIM, EITHER. MAYBE *THE FORCE* REALLY *IS* THEIR ONLY HOPE.

LUKE ISN'T IN FIRING RANGE, NOT YET, AND THE TIE FIGHTERS ARE STILL ON HIS TAIL. BUT HE *TURNS OFF* HIS COMPUTER AND FOCUSES HIS INSTINCTS, TRYING TO *FEEL THE FORCE* AROUND HIM.

THEN THE ODD-SHAPED TIE MOVES CLOSER. A LASER BLAST *HITS* ARTOO. THE NEXT ONE WILL HIT HIS X-WING SQUARELY, LUKE REALIZES WITH DESPAIR. HE'S SO *CLOSE,* BUT—

AS IF BY *MAGIC*, ONE OF THE TIE FIGHTERS FOLLOWING LUKE *EXPLODES* IN A BURST OF FLAME.

THE EXPLOSION SENDS THE SECOND TIE INTO THE ODD-SHAPED FIGHTER, CAUSING IT TO *SPIN* OUT OF THE TRENCH AND *INTO SPACE.*

CHOOOM

SHOOOM

PEW

THEN *HAN'S VOICE* COMES THROUGH LUKE'S COMM: "YOU'RE ALL CLEAR, KID. LET'S BLOW THIS THING AND GO HOME!"

HAN SAVED MY LIFE, LUKE THINKS. THE SMUGGLER HAS GIVEN THE REBEL CAUSE ONE *FINAL CHANCE* FOR VICTORY

LUKE REACHES OUT WITH HIS FEELINGS, AND THIS TIME HE *KNOWS* WHAT TO DO. HE AIMS, AND WHEN IT FEELS RIGHT, HE PULLS THE TRIGGERS.

THE TORPEDOES BURST FROM THEIR HOUSINGS AND SLIP INTO THE EXHAUST PORT. *BULL'S-EYE!*

HAN'S CHEER RINGS THROUGH THE COMM. "GREAT SHOT, KID. THAT WAS ONE IN A MILLION!"

AND LUKE HEARS *BEN'S VOICE* AGAIN: REMEMBER, THE FORCE WILL BE WITH YOU, ALWAYS.

LUKE PULLS HIS
X-WING UPWARD AT *FULL
THROTTLE*, OUT OF THE
TRENCH AND INTO SPACE,
WHERE THE *MILLENNIUM
FALCON* AND WEDGE'S
X-WING ARE WAITING.

THE TORPEDOES ARE NOW
MOVING THROUGH THE
DEATH STAR AND WILL SOON
REACH *THE REACTOR.*
FIVE, LUKE COUNTS. FOUR.
THREE. TWO. ONE.

THOO

THE *DEATH STAR EXPLODES* INTO A BILLION FRAGMENTS.

WHEN LUKE CLIMBS FROM HIS X-WING BACK ON THE BASE, A *CHEERING CROWD* SURROUNDS HIM. PRINCESS LEIA THROWS HER ARMS AROUND HIM AND HUGS HIM TIGHT. THEN HAN DASHES UP AND JOINS IN THEIR VICTORY CELEBRATION.

"I KNEW YOU'D COME BACK!" LUKE CRIES.

HAN LAUGHS. "I WASN'T GONNA LET YOU GET ALL THE CREDIT AND TAKE ALL THE REWARD!"

BUT DESPITE WHAT HAN SAYS, HIS ACTIONS PROVE HIS FRIENDS ARE *MORE IMPORTANT* TO HIM THAN MONEY. HAN PUT HIS LIFE IN DANGER TO SAVE THEM ALL.

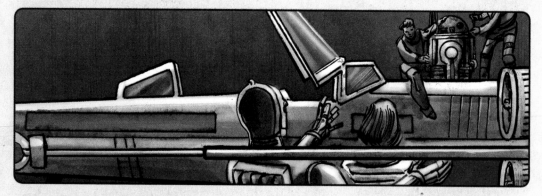

BRAVE LITTLE ARTOO IS LOWERED FROM THE X-WING, LOOKING MUCH *WORSE* THAN THE DAY LUKE'S UNCLE BOUGHT HIM. THREEPIO GAZES AT HIS BEST FRIEND IN *HORROR*. "ARTOO, CAN YOU HEAR ME?" HE CRIES. "SAY SOMETHING!"

LUKE WILL ALWAYS MISS HIS BEST FRIEND, BIGGS, SO HE UNDERSTANDS HOW THREEPIO FEELS. HE *ASSURES* THE GOLDEN DROID THAT ARTOO WILL SOON BE AS GOOD AS NEW.

SOON IT IS TIME TO FORMALLY *CELEBRATE* THEIR MAGNIFICENT VICTORY.

AS LUKE STANDS AT ATTENTION BEFORE THE ASSEMBLED REBELS, HIS HEART SWELLS. *TOGETHER,* THEY DESTROYED THE EMPIRE'S MOST POWERFUL WEAPON. LEIA DELIVERED THE PLANS, AND HAN AND CHEWIE BLEW AWAY THE TIE FIGHTERS, GIVING LUKE THE CHANCE TO DEMOLISH THE DEATH STAR.

DESPITE ALL HE HAS LOST, LUKE SKYWALKER FEELS *HAPPY,* AS THOUGH HE HAS A *NEW PURPOSE* AND A *NEW HOPE* FOR THE *FUTURE.*

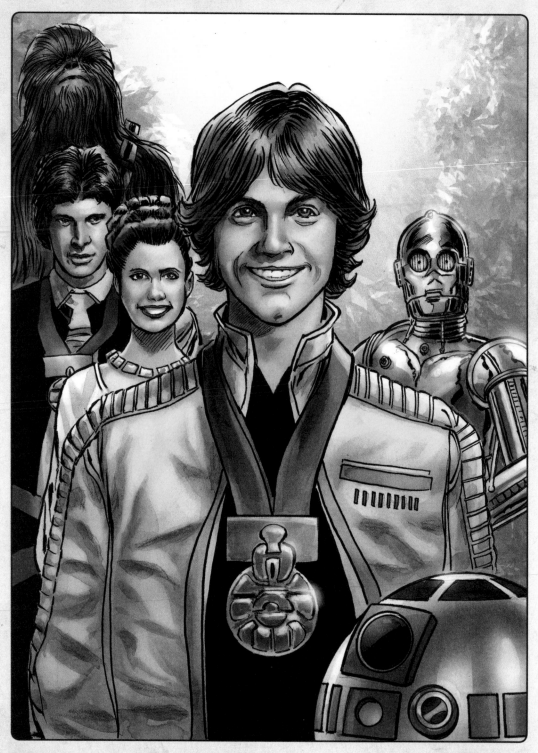

IT'S LIKE *BEN* TOLD ME, LUKE THINKS AS HE LOOKS OUT AT THE CHEERING REBELS. *THE FORCE WILL BE WITH ME, ALWAYS.*